Published in Moonstone
by Rupa Publications India Pvt. Ltd 2025
7/16, Ansari Road, Daryaganj
New Delhi 110002

Sales centres:
Bengaluru Chennai
Hyderabad Jaipur Kathmandu
Kolkata Mumbai Prayagraj

Copyright © Rupa Publications India Pvt. Ltd 2025

All rights reserved.

No part of this publication may be reproduced, transmitted,
or stored in a retrieval system, in any form or by any means,
electronic, mechanical, photocopying, recording or otherwise,
without the prior permission of the publisher.

P-ISBN: 978-93-6156-185-6
E-ISBN: 978-93-6156-506-9

First impression 2025

10 9 8 7 6 5 4 3 2 1

Printed in India
This book is sold subject to the condition that it shall not,
by way of trade or otherwise, be lent, resold, hired out, or otherwise
circulated, without the publisher's prior consent, in any form of binding
or cover other than that in which it is published.

1. **Complete each sentence with the correct article (a or an).**

1. _____ umbrella is useful on _____ rainy day.
2. My sister bought _____ iguana, _____ hamster, and _____ rabbit from the pet store.
3. Henry packed _____ jacket, _____ pair of gloves, and _____ hat for the trip.
4. A squirrel built _____ home inside _____ old oak tree.
5. _____ elephant and _____ antelope were seen near _____ watering hole.
6. James had _____ omelette and _____ slice of toast for breakfast.
7. We waited for _____ hour before catching _____ bus to the city.

2. **Do as instructed.**

a. Write four things you notice when walking outside.

i. _____ iii. _____

ii. _____ iv. _____

b. List four ingredients that are often used in home.

i. _____ iii. _____

ii. _____ iv. _____

c. Name four objects that help students learn effectively.

i. _____ iii. _____

ii. _____ iv. _____

3. Do as instructed.

a. Write four plants or trees that you find beautiful.

i. _____   iii. _____

ii. _____   iv. _____

b. List four animals that live in forests or jungles.

i. _____   iii. _____

ii. _____   iv. _____

c. Name four animals commonly raised by farmers.

i. _____   iii. _____

ii. _____   iv. _____

4. Choose the correct verb to complete each sentence: 'has' or 'have'.

i.   The dog _____ a long tail.

ii. They _____ three bicycles.

iii. She _____ a new notebook.

iv. We _____ a holiday next week.

5. Replace the underlined nouns with pronouns.

Riya has a pet cat. <u>Riya</u> takes <u>the cat</u> to the park every evening. <u>Riya's cat</u> loves to play with <u>the children</u>. Sometimes, <u>the children</u> bring treats for <u>Riya's cat</u>.

_____ _____ _____ _____ _____ _____

6. Rewrite the following phrases into complete sentences.

i. A big, fluffy cat on the couch.

_____

ii. Running towards the finish line.

_____

iii. The children played outside all evening.

_____

7. Match the words in the list with the blanks in the sentences.

Words:
stormy   brave   hidden   rough   legendary   salty

a. The pirates sailed through the _____ sea.

b. A _____ map led them to the treasure.

c. The captain was a _____ leader of the crew.

d. The water tasted _____ because it was from the ocean.

e. Many _____ pirates have been written about in books.

8. Fill in the blanks with 'was' or 'were'.

a. The detective _____ following a secret clue.

b. There _____ footprints on the muddy road.

c. The stolen painting _____ found in an old mansion.

d. All the suspects _____ questioned by the police.

e. _____ the case solved last night?

9. Fill in the blanks using 'your' or 'you're'.

i. _____ going to love this movie!

ii. Don't forget to bring _____ homework.

iii. I think _____ very talented.

iv. _____ cat is sleeping under the table.

v. _____ the best friend I could ever ask for!

vi. Is this _____ book or mine?

10. Fill in the blanks using 'had' or 'has'.

i. He _____ a wonderful time at the fair yesterday.

ii. This shop _____ the best cakes in town.

iii. We _____ a great holiday last year.

iv. The cat _____ blue eyes.

v. She _____ a very kind heart.

11. Rewrite the sentences with correct capital letters and punctuation.

i. the little girl has a doll _____

ii. did you hear that noise _____

iii. can we go to the park tomorrow _____

iv. he is watching television now _____

v. where did you put my keys _____

vi. oh no i forgot my homework _____

12. Rearrange the words to make meaningful sentences.

a. fun, having, we, are, today.

_____

b. bright, the, sun, is, shining.

_____

c. a, eats, banana, monkey, the.

_____

d. slowly, walks, the, tortoise.

_____

e. beautiful, a, garden, has, she.

_____

f. listening, music, love, I, to.

_____

13. Choose the correct word from the list to complete the sentences:

soft   clever   deep   warm   noisy   quick

i. The baby has a very _____ blanket.

ii. That was a _____ idea!

iii. Be careful! The river is very _____.

iv. It was a _____ day, perfect for a picnic.

v. The students were too _____ during the lesson.

vi. She gave me a _____ response.

14. Fill in the blanks with 'do' or 'does'.

i. _____ you like ice cream?

ii. She _____ not understand the question.

iii. _____ your parents know about your trip?

iv. He _____ his homework before dinner.

v. _____ we need to bring anything to the party?

15. Complete the sentences with proper nouns.

i. _____ is the capital of France.

ii. My best friend's name is _____.

iii. _____ is my favourite book.

iv. The _____ River is the longest in the world.

v. I visited _____ last summer.

16. Choose the correct quantifier 'much' or 'many'.

i. How _____ sugar do you need?

ii. She has so _____ books in her library.

iii. There isn't _____ water left in the bottle.

iv. We saw _____ birds in the park today.

v. There wasn't _____ noise in the classroom.

17. Rewrite the sentences with proper capitalisation.

i. my father and i went to new york.

   _____

ii. she bought a dress from london.

   _____

iii. they saw the eiffel tower in paris.

   _____

iv. we are reading a book by william shakespeare.

   _____

v. tomorrow is sunday.

   _____

18. Complete the sentences with 'this', 'that', 'these', or 'those'.

i. _____ apple is very sweet.

ii. _____ books on the table belong to me.

iii. Is _____ your car parked outside?

iv. _____ flowers are blooming beautifully.

v. _____ chair over there is broken.

19. Rearrange the words into correct sentences.

i. on, shines, the, brightly, sun.

_____

ii. plays, park, the, in, she.

_____

iii. car, blue, is, the, very, fast.

_____

iv. dog, brown, has, tail, a, fluffy.

_____

v. book, interesting, an, read, I.

_____

20. Find the best word from the list to complete the blanks.

Words:
happy   lazy   sharp   small   friendly   rough

i. The kitten is very _____ and loves to play.

ii. He always smiles because he is a _____ person.

iii. The pencil has a _____ tip.

iv. This towel feels very _____.

v. She found a _____ shell on the beach.

vi. My brother is _____ and never wants to do his homework.

21. Fill in the blanks with 'is' or 'are'.

i. The stars _____ shining brightly in the sky.

ii. There _____ a spaceship ready for takeoff.

iii. Astronauts _____ trained before they go to space.

iv. The moon _____ visible from my telescope.

v. _____ those aliens real?

22. Rearrange the words to make sentences about space.

1. galaxy, Milky Way, in, the, Earth, is, the.

   _____

2. stars, millions, twinkle, night, at, of.

   _____

3. around, planets, Sun, the, move.

   _____

4. is, a, space, exciting, topic.

   _____

5. Neil Armstrong, on, moon, walked, the.

   _____

23. Insert the correct option from the choices below.

Words:
bright   round   far   huge   dark   silent

i.   The moon looks very _____ in the sky.

ii. Space is a vast and _____ place.

iii. Planets are _____ objects floating in space.

iv. Stars are _____ from Earth.

v.   The spaceship floated in the _____ silence of space.

24. Fill in the blanks with 'was' or 'were'.

i.   The lions _____ sleeping under the tree.

ii. There _____ a huge elephant near the river.

iii. The monkeys _____ jumping from one tree to another.

iv. It _____ a beautiful morning in the jungle.

v.   _____ the snake hiding in the bushes?

25. Complete the sentences with 'their' or 'there'.

i.   The tigers were resting in _____ den over _____.

ii. _____ were many birds sitting on _____ favourite tree.

iii. We saw elephants playing with _____ trunks.

iv. The guide took us to a place where _____ was a rare flower.

v.   Some monkeys were playing with _____ baby brothers.

26. Fill in each sentence using a suitable word from the given set.

Words:
fierce   gentle   slippery   wild   tall   colourful

i. The giraffe has a very _____ neck.

ii. Parrots are _____ birds with bright feathers.

iii. The leopard is a _____ hunter.

iv. The river was full of _____ fish.

v. The elephant is a _____ giant of the jungle.

27. Fill in the blanks with 'do' or 'does'.

i. _____ the prince have a golden sword?

ii. _____ fairies grant wishes?

iii. The queen _____ not allow anyone to enter the castle.

iv. _____ you believe in magic?

v. The elves _____ their work quietly at night.

28. Rearrange the words to make sentences about fairy tales.

i. castle, the, princess, in, lived, magical, a.

   _____

ii. dragon, fierce, the, fire, breathed.

   _____

29. Which is your favourite subject and why?

_____

_____

_____

30. Pick a word that best fits the blank space.

Words:

golden   brave   wicked   tiny   enchanted   mysterious

i.   The knight was _____ and fought the dragon.

ii. The fairy granted the child a _____ wish.

iii. The witch had a _____ laugh.

iv. A _____ door appeared in the forest.

v.   The prince found a _____ key under the tree.

31. Fill in the blanks with 'is' or 'are'.

i.   The flowers _____ blooming beautifully.

ii. There _____ a butterfly sitting on the flower.

iii. The birds _____ chirping in the trees.

iv. The sun _____ shining brightly today.

v.   _____ those tulips in your garden?

32. Rearrange the words to make sentences about spring.

i. flowers, spring, in, beautiful, are.

_____

ii. playing, birds, trees, the, in, are.

_____

iii. new, plants, farmers, in, fields, grow.

_____

iv. air, fresh, the, is, and, breezy.

_____

v. in, start, when, March, spring, does?

_____

33. Choose one word from the list to make each sentence complete.

Words:
bright   fresh   soft   cool   tiny   buzzing

i. The air feels _____ after the rain.

ii. A bee is _____ around the flowers.

iii. The baby rabbits are so _____!

iv. The sky looks _____ and blue today.

v. We felt a _____ breeze in the morning.

34. Fill in the blanks with 'was' or 'were'.

i. The pyramids _____ built by the ancient Egyptians.

ii. The Great Wall of China _____ a massive structure.

iii. There _____ many soldiers in the Roman army.

iv. The ancient city of Troy _____ famous in myths.

v. The kings and queens _____ powerful rulers.

35. Complete the sentences with 'their' or 'there'.

a. The warriors protected _____ land over _____.

b. _____ were many treasures hidden in _____ palace.

c. The knights rode on _____ horses across the battlefield.

d. The scholars wrote _____ knowledge on scrolls kept _____.

e. _____ was an ancient library where they stored _____ books.

36. Select the word that makes the sentence meaningful.

Words:
mighty   wise   ancient   strong   legendary   golden

a. The king had a _____ sword.

b. The pyramids are _____ structures.

c. The warrior was _____ and brave.

d. Many _____ stories are told about lost cities.

e. The philosopher gave a _____ speech.

37. Fill in the blanks with 'do' or 'does'.

a. _____ lions hunt at night?

b. _____ elephants live in the jungle?

c. The tiger _____ not like loud noises.

d. _____ you know that giraffes have long tongues?

e. _____ zebras run very fast?

38. Rearrange the words to make sentences about a safari.

a. lions, the, sleeping, are, under, trees, the.

_____

b. across, zebra, river, a, crossed, the.

_____

c. wild, the, jungle, deep, animals, live, in.

_____

d. chasing, cheetah, a, deer, was, fast, a

_____

e. in, baby, with, was, walking, its, elephant, mother, the.

_____

39. Write the most appropriate word from the box in the blank.

Words:
fierce   tall   fast   spotted   powerful   gentle

a. The cheetah is the most _____ animal in the jungle.

b. The giraffe is very _____ and can reach the tallest trees.

c. Leopards have _____ fur with black spots.

d. The lion is a _____ predator in the wild.

e. Elephants are _____ but also very strong.

40. Rearrange the words to make sentences about mystery.

a. detective, found, the, secret, a, message.

_____

b. mystery, solving, difficult, mother, the, was, it.

_____

c. looked, suspect, the, very, nervous.

_____

d. disappeared, valuable, a, diamond.

_____

e. the, door, creaked, in, the, middle, of, night, the.

_____

41. Fill in the blanks with 'is' or 'are'.

a. The pirate ship _____ sailing across the ocean.

b. The treasure chests _____ filled with gold.

c. There _____ an island on the horizon!

d. The pirates _____ looking for hidden treasure.

e. _____ this your pirate hat?

42. Rearrange the words to make sentences about pirates.

a. sailing, the, waves, pirate, on, ship, was.

_____

b. treasure, found, they, a, golden, chest.

_____

c. map, looking, the, was, at, captain, the.

_____

d. parrot, on, pirate's, shoulder, sat, a.

_____

e. the, across, ocean, sailing, were, pirates, the.

_____

43. Add the missing word from the selection given below.

Words:
suspicious   dark   secret   hidden   clever   missing

a. The detective found a _____ tunnel under the house.

b. The suspect gave a _____ alibi.

c. The old book contained a _____ message.

d. The jewels were still _____ inside the cupboard.

e. There was something _____ about his behaviour.

44. Help the sentence make sense by choosing the right word.

Words:
enchanted   magical   mysterious   ancient   golden   powerful

a. The fairy granted a _____ wish.

b. A _____ spell turned the prince into a frog.

c. The knight found a _____ shield in the cave.

d. A _____ castle stood deep in the forest.

e. The wizard carried an _____ book of spells.

45. Fill in the blanks with 'is' or 'are'.

a. The wizard _____ casting a powerful spell.

b. There _____ dragons flying over the castle.

c. The enchanted book _____ glowing with blue light.

d. Fairies _____ dancing in the moonlight.

e. _____ this your magic wand?

46. Rearrange the words to make sentences about fantasy.

a. wizard, powerful, a, spell, cast, the.

_____

b. land, fairy, creatures, magical, lived, in, the.

_____

c. shining, sword, golden, a, found, knight, the.

_____

d. dragon, fire, the, breathing, was.

_____

e. castle, behind, mountains, the, stood, enchanted.

_____

47. Rearrange the words to make sentences about science.

a. the, scientist, discovered, cure, a, disease, for, the.

_____

b. experiment, test, the, was, successful.

_____

c. electricity, Thomas Edison, invented.

_____

d. discovered, penicillin, Alexander Fleming.

_____

e. space, astronauts, outer, explore.

_____

48. Circle or write the word that best fits in each sentence.

Words:
intelligent   innovative   robotic   advanced   scientific   electric

a. The robot had a _____ arm.

b. Scientists use _____ methods to study diseases.

c. Many _____ inventions changed the world.

d. Thomas Edison created the first _____ light bulb.

e. The spaceship had an _____ navigation system.

49. Rearrange the words to make sentences about horror.

i. dark, in, creaked, the, door, the, night.

_____

ii. ran, ghost, a, when, they, screamed, saw, they, and.

_____

iii. haunted, old, an, lived, spirit, house, in, the.

_____

iv. horror, the, terrifying, was, film, very.

_____

v. moved, chair, nobody, was, it, though.

_____

50. Complete the sentences by choosing the correct words from the options.

Words:
eerie   creepy   mysterious   haunted   terrifying   shadowy

i. The house had an _____ atmosphere that gave me chills.

ii. A _____ figure appeared in the mirror.

iii. Strange, _____ footsteps were heard at midnight.

iv. The old castle is said to be _____ by ghosts.

v. The horror movie was so _____ that I couldn't sleep!

51. Fill in the blanks with 'is' or 'are'.

i. Superman _____ known for his strength.

ii. The villains _____ planning their next attack.

iii. There _____ a new superhero in town!

iv. Superheroes _____ always ready to fight for justice.

v. _____ this your superhero mask?

52. Fill in the blanks with 'do' or 'does'.

a. _____ scientists study space?

b. _____ you know how a rocket works?

c. The microscope _____ not work properly.

d. _____ we need batteries for the experiment?

e. The machine _____ all the calculations for us.

53. Fill in the blanks with 'was' or 'were'.

i. The old mansion _____ abandoned for years.

ii. There _____ eerie whispers coming from the basement.

iii. A ghostly shadow _____ seen in the window.

iv. The candles _____ flickering without any wind.

v. _____ the haunted house real or just a legend?

54. Rearrange the words to make sentences about superheroes.

i. powers, super, has, hero, a, special.

_____

ii. the, villain, evil, was, planning, attack, an.

_____

iii. buildings, leaped, tall, hero, over, the.

_____

iv. citizens, rescue, superhero, the, to, arrived, the.

_____

v. secret, his, superhero, identity, revealed, the.

_____

55. Look at the list and decide which word completes each sentence.

Words:
powerful   fearless   heroic   legendary   unstoppable   cunning

i. The superhero was _____ and never backed down from a fight.

ii. The villain's plan was _____ but the hero outsmarted him.

iii. Spider-Man is a _____ character known worldwide.

iv. The Flash is _____ and can move at the speed of light.

v. The battle between good and evil was truly _____.

56. Fill in the blanks with 'do' or 'does'.

i. _____ time machines really exist?

ii. _____ you believe in alternate universes?

iii. The scientist _____ not know how to return to the present.

iv. _____ we need a special device to travel through time?

v. This portal _____ not look stable!

57. Rearrange the words to make sentences about time travel.

i. past, went, the, machine, into, time, the.

   _____

ii. strange, a, met, future, traveler, I, from.

   _____

iii. ancient, visited, the, they, civilization.

   _____

iv. changed, one, timeline, new, created, event, a.

_____

v. back, wanted, get, present, to, they, the.

_____

58. Use one of the words from the box to fill each blank correctly.

Words:
futuristic   ancient   advanced
unknown   paradoxical   impossible

a. The scientist stepped into an _____ civilization.

b. The time machine had an _____ design.

c. He discovered an _____ planet far from Earth.

d. Time loops can create _____ situations.

e. Some say travelling faster than light is _____.

59. Fill in the blanks with 'was' or 'were'.

a. Zeus _____ the king of the gods.

b. There _____ twelve Olympian gods in Greek mythology.

c. The temple _____ built to honour the goddess Athena.

d. Heroes like Hercules _____ known for their strength.

e. _____ Poseidon the god of the sea?

60. Rearrange the words to make sentences proper sense.

a. powerful, gods, the, ruled, sky, the.

_____

b. carried, mighty, a, Thor, hammer.

_____

c. Hades, underworld, the, ruled, the, in.

_____

d. legends, heroes, fought, great, battles.

_____

e. goddess, beauty, of, was, Aphrodite, the.

_____

61. Choose a word from the options to complete each sentence.

Words:
divine   legendary   immortal   mighty   mystical   heroic

a. The gods were _____ beings who never aged.

b. Hercules completed many _____ tasks.

c. The sword was said to have _____ powers.

d. Zeus was a _____ ruler of Mount Olympus.

e. Many _____ stories were told about warriors of the past.

62. Fill in the blanks with 'is' or 'are'.

a. The ocean _____ full of mysteries.

b. There _____ colourful fish swimming in the coral reef.

c. A giant whale _____ spotted near the island.

d. The deep-sea creatures _____ glowing in the dark.

e. _____ this an ancient shipwreck?

63. Rearrange the words to make sentences about the ocean.

a. deep, the, the, whale, dived, into, sea.

   _____

b. underwater, glowing, creatures, amazing, saw, we.

   _____

c. lost, treasure, pirate, the, in, the, found, cave.

   _____

d. swam, the, fish, coral, through, reef, the.

   _____

e. waves, crashed, shore, the, on, the.

   _____

64. Each sentence needs a word—select it from the list provided.

Words:
mysterious   shimmering   deep   vast   hidden   magical

i. The ocean is a _____ place full of unknown species.

ii. Sunlight made the waves look _____ in the morning.

iii. The diver explored the _____ underwater cave.

iv. There are _____ treasures buried under the sea.

v. The ocean is so _____ that humans have only explored a small part of it.

65. Rearrange the words to make sentences about the future.

i. flying, cars, city, futuristic, in, a, were.
   _____

ii. robots, daily, helped, tasks, humans, with.
   _____

iii. holograms, news, delivering, people, the, to, were.
   _____

iv. energy, from, buildings, sun, power, the, took.
   _____

v. advanced, system, city, security, had, an, the.
   _____

66. Find the missing word from the list to complete the following.

Words:
advanced   intelligent   robotic   digital   futuristic   high-tech

i. The city was filled with _____ buildings made of glass and steel.

ii. _____ assistants helped people with their daily tasks.

iii. Cars in the future will have _____ self-driving systems.

iv. The world was turning into a completely _____ society.

v. Scientists created an _____ AI that could think like a human.

67. Fill in the blanks with 'was' or 'were'.

i. The woolly mammoth _____ covered in thick fur.

ii. There _____ several herds roaming the icy plains.

iii. A sudden change in climate _____ the reason they vanished.

iv. The remains _____ found beneath layers of frozen soil.

v. _____ the sabre-toothed tiger a meat-eater?

68. Rearrange the words to make sentences about dinosaurs.

1. dinosaurs, ruled, the, Earth, years, million, ago.

   _____

2. had, spikes, long, Stegosaurus, back, its, on.

   _____

3. Velociraptor, was, hunter, a, fast.

   _____

4. flying, huge, in, Pterodactyl, the, sky, was, a.

   _____

5. fossils, discovered, scientists, bones, buried, of.

   _____

69. Let the sentence make sense—add the right word from the group below.

Words:
prehistoric   enormous   deadly   ancient   terrifying   extinct

1. The dinosaurs lived in _____ times.

2. The Spinosaurus was an _____ predator.

3. The T-Rex had _____ teeth for hunting.

4. Fossils are remains of _____ creatures.

5. Dinosaurs became _____ after a massive disaster.

70. Fill in the blanks with 'is' or 'are'.

1. The spaceship _____ ready for launch.

2. There _____ mysterious signals coming from deep space.

3. An alien species _____ discovered on a distant planet.

4. The stars _____ shining brightly in the galaxy.

5. _____ this the fastest spaceship in the universe?

71. Rearrange the words to make sentences about space wars.

1. battle, in, space, fought, was, a.

   _____

2. planets, war, across, the, spread.

   _____

3. fired, lasers, spaceship, the, enemy, at, the.

   _____

4. controlled, powerful, the, galaxy, overlords.

   _____

5. human, mission, defend, was, Earth, to, the.

   _____

72. Fill in the blanks with 'do' or 'does'.

i. _____ robots control the city?

ii. _____ flying cars exist in the future?

iii. The scientist _____ not understand the new AI system.

iv. _____ we need permission to enter the smart city?

v. The skyscrapers _____ not have traditional windows anymore.

73. Match each word with the correct blank in the sentence.

Words:
galactic   powerful   futuristic   alien   dangerous   high-speed

1. The spaceship used _____ weapons to attack.

2. The enemy had a fleet of _____ battle cruisers.

3. The Earth was under attack by _____ invaders.

4. The spaceship had _____ engines that could travel at light speed.

5. The war spread across the entire _____ empire.

74. Fill in the blanks with 'do' or 'does'.

1. _____ fairies really exist?

2. _____ you believe in talking trees?

3. The unicorn _____ not come out during the day.

4. _____ elves have magical powers?

5. The glowing mushrooms _____ not harm anyone.

75. Rearrange the words to make sentences about an enchanted forest.

1. hidden, deep, the, in, forest, fairies, live.

   _____

2. trees, whispered, ancient, secrets, the.

   _____

3. discovered, glowing, lake, a, magical, we.

   _____

4. spell, cast, wizard, an, a, powerful, a.

   _____

5. enchanted, into, she, woods, wandered, the.

   _____

76. Select a word from the box and write it in the correct space.

Words:
mystical   glowing   ancient   enchanted   whispering   magical

1. The fairy held a _____ wand in her hand.

2. The lake had _____ water that changed colours.

3. The forest was filled with _____ creatures.

4. The trees were old and _____ with age.

5. The wind was _____ through the leaves.

77. Fill in the blanks with 'was' or 'were'.

1. The lost city of Atlantis _____ said to have sunk into the ocean.

2. There _____ many treasures hidden beneath the ruins.

3. The pyramid _____ built by an ancient civilization.

4. The statues _____ covered in moss and vines.

5. _____ this the entrance to the lost temple?

78. Rearrange the words to make sentences about lost cities.

1. buried, city, was, the, desert, under, the.

   _____

2. temple, ancient, discovered, explorers, an.

   _____

3. secrets, hidden, many, within, walls, were, the.

   _____

4. jungle, ruins, covered, the, of, lost, kingdom.

   _____

5. map, treasure, led, old, us, to, city, the, the.

   _____

79. Read carefully and fill in the blanks with words from the choices given.

Words:
hidden   mysterious   ancient   forgotten   legendary   golden

1. The ruins contained _____ symbols carved into stone.

2. A _____ kingdom was believed to exist beyond the mountains.

3. The explorer found a _____ city deep in the jungle.

4. The tomb held _____ treasures untouched for centuries.

5. The lost civilization had been _____ for thousands of years.

80. Fill in the blanks with 'is' or 'are'.

1. The Arctic _____ covered in ice and snow.

2. There _____ many polar bears in this region.

3. A frozen shipwreck _____ found under the ice.

4. The glaciers _____ melting due to climate change.

5. _____ this the coldest place on Earth?

81. Rearrange the words to make sentences about arctic explorations.

1. sled, pulled, dogs, the, explorers, by, were.
   _____

2. frozen, river, the, across, walked, they.
   _____

3. iceberg, a, large, floating, saw, we.
   _____

4. Arctic, freezing, the, temperatures, had.
   _____

5. compass, their, with, directions, checked, explorers.
   _____

82. Use your vocabulary skills to complete the blanks with the right words.

Words:
freezing   icy   slippery   harsh   brave   remote

1. The journey through the Arctic was _____ and difficult.
2. The explorers walked carefully on the _____ surface.
3. The temperatures were _____ below zero.
4. Only the most _____ adventurers dared to travel here.
5. The research station was located in a _____ area far from civilization.

bonus challenge:
write a diary entry from an arctic explorer, using at least three of these words!

83. Fill in the blanks with 'do' or 'does'.

1. _____ mermaids really exist?

2. _____ you know how deep the ocean is?

3. The diver _____ not see the sunken ship at first.

4. _____ sea creatures communicate with each other?

5. The submarine _____ not need human control.

84. Rearrange the words to make sentences about underwater mysteries.

1. beneath, ocean, shipwreck, a, the, was, hidden.

   _____

2. glowing, jellyfish, saw, deep, a, we.

   _____

3. mermaid, legends, mysterious, tell, of, a.

   _____

4. scientists, creatures, discovered, new, deep, in, the, ocean.

   _____

5. bubbles, swam, among, the, fish.

   _____

85. Can you find the perfect word to complete each sentence? Use the list!

Words:
deep   glowing   mysterious   silent   unknown   hidden

1. The ocean is full of _____ creatures.

2. A strange, _____ cave was discovered near the seabed.

3. The fish had _____ markings that lit up in the dark.

4. The divers found a _____ passage leading to the wreck.

5. The water was calm and _____ as they sank deeper.

86. Fill in the blanks with 'is' or 'are'.

1. The robot _____ programmed to follow commands.

2. There _____ many different types of robots in factories.

3. A new AI system _____ being tested in the lab.

4. The robotic arms _____ assembling cars on the production line.

5. _____ this machine fully automated?

87. Rearrange the words to make sentences about robots.

1. robots, designed, are, perform, tasks, to.

   _____

2. controlled, a, by, computer, robot, is.

   _____

3. assistant, an, virtual, intelligent, uses, AI.

   _____

4. future, the, in, replace, jobs, some, robots, will.

   _____

5. programmed, was, complete, the, robot, the, task, to.

   _____

88. Use the correct word from the box to finish each sentence.

Words:
automated   intelligent   futuristic   mechanical   advanced   digital

1. Factories use _____ machines to build products.

2. Scientists developed an _____ AI system to assist doctors.

3. The city had a _____ design with self-driving cars.

4. Robots have _____ arms that can lift heavy objects.

5. The world is shifting toward a more _____ economy.

89. Fill in the blanks with 'was' or 'were'.

1. The island _____ surrounded by crystal-clear water.

2. There _____ ancient ruins hidden in the jungle.

3. A treasure map _____ found inside a dusty chest.

4. The sailors _____ stranded on the island for weeks.

5. _____ this the lost island of legend?

90. Rearrange the words to make sentences about secret islands.

1. discovered, map, treasure, a, old, the, sailors.

   _____

2. island, hidden, secret, a, in, ocean, the.

   _____

3. jungle, through, explorers, the, walked.

   _____

4. waves, crashed, shore, the, upon.

   _____

5. golden, chest, treasure, the, opened, they.

   _____

91. Find the best word from the list to complete the blanks.

Words:
hidden   tropical   mysterious   golden   deserted   legendary

1. The island was a _____ place with no human life.

2. The sailors searched for the _____ treasure.

3. A _____ jungle covered most of the land.

4. The legend spoke of a _____ kingdom lost in time.

5. A _____ cave was found beneath the cliffs.

92. Fill in the blanks with 'do' or 'does'.

1. _____ knights still exist today?

2. _____ you know how castles were built?

3. The king _____ not allow strangers inside the fortress.

4. _____ warriors wear armour in battle?

5. The drawbridge _____ not open without a key.

93. Rearrange the words to make sentences about medieval castles.

1. castle, the, surrounded, was, walls, by, strong.

   _____

2. knights, fought, battle, in, bravely, the, the.

   _____

3. swords, shields, their, warriors, carried, and.

   _____

4. queen, in, the, castle, lived, the, grand.

   _____

5. torch, guided, light, dark, the, hallways, through, the.

   _____

94. Insert the correct option from the choices below.

Words:
grand   ancient   fortified   noble   royal   majestic

1. The king sat on a _____ throne made of gold.

2. The castle was _____ with tall stone walls.

3. The knights fought to protect their _____ ruler.

4. A _____ sword was displayed in the great hall.

5. The _____ towers overlooked the entire kingdom.

95. Fill in the blanks with 'is' or 'are'.

1. The superhero academy _____ hidden from the public.

2. There _____ many young heroes learning new powers.

3. A powerful villain _____ trying to sneak into the academy.

4. The students _____ training in the danger room.

5. _____ this your superhero suit?

96. Rearrange the words to make sentences about superhero academies.

1. superheroes, their, control, must, learn, powers, to.

   _____

2. mentor, hero, young, training, was, a, their.

   _____

3. villains, city, the, protect, heroes, from, must.

   _____

4. secret, a, had, the, academy, location.

   _____

5. powers, incredible, had, students, the.

   _____

97. Fill in each sentence using a suitable word from the given set.

Words:
heroic powerful fearless invisible superhuman unstoppable

1. The young hero had _____ strength.

2. Some superheroes can turn _____ and disappear.

3. The team remained _____ in the face of danger.

4. The villain thought he was _____, but he was defeated.

5. A true hero is always _____ and fights for justice.

98. Fill in the blanks with 'was' or 'were'.

1. The underground city _____ discovered beneath the ruins.

2. There _____ tunnels leading to different parts of the city.

3. A strange light _____ glowing in the darkness.

4. The ancient people _____ hiding from their enemies.

5. _____ this the entrance to the hidden civilization?

99. Rearrange the words to make sentences about underground cities.

1. tunnels, dark, deep, stretched, far, and.

   _____

2. explorers, city, found, hidden, a, beneath.

   _____

3. glowing, crystals, underground, the, lit, caves.

   _____

4. lost, years, for, hidden, had, city, the, been.

   _____

5. safe, kept, underground, people, their, treasures.

   _____

100. Pick a word that best fits the blank space.

Words:
hidden   mysterious   ancient   glowing   secret   lost)

1. The underground city had _____ passageways leading everywhere.

2. Scientists found a _____ artifact buried beneath the ruins.

3. The cave walls were covered in _____ symbols.

4. A _____ light flickered inside the tunnel.

5. The people who once lived here are now _____ to history.

101. Write your own clever riddle and see if someone can guess the answer.

Example:

"I have four legs, but I'm not alive.
I can hold you up when you sit inside. What am I?"

Answer: A chair

Your riddle:

_____

_____

Answer:

_____

Tip:
Use clues that describe shape, use, and mystery without naming the object!

_____

102. Rewrite each sentence in past and future tenses.

1. Emma reads a book.

- Past: _____

- Future: _____

2. The dog runs in the park.

- Past: _____

- Future: _____

103. Choose the correct word from the list to complete the sentences.

Words:
enchanted   dusty   ancient   glowing   floating   forbidden

1. The wizard opened an _____ book filled with forgotten spells.

2. The librarian warned us not to touch the _____ section.

3. The candlelight made the golden letters appear _____.

4. The shelves were filled with _____ tomes covered in cobwebs.

5. A mysterious book was _____ in mid-air, turning its own pages.

104. Circle the picture on each line that has the same meaning as the word.

Window	window	lemon slice	sailboat
Car	mushroom	green car	candy
Carrot	picture frame	clock	carrot
Orange	orange	donut	helicopter
Envelope	cupcake	envelope	cherries

105. Rearrange the words to make sentences about steampunk inventions.

1. powered, machine, a, by, steam, ran.
   _____

2. golden, gears, huge, were, turning.
   _____

3. scientist, new, designed, machine, the, a.
   _____

4. inventions, steam, powered, changed, the, world.
   _____

5. flying, goggles, wore, their, inventors, machines, tested.
   _____

106. Choose the correct word from the list to complete the sentences.

Words:
mechanical   steam-powered   intricate
brass   futuristic   gear-driven

1. The city was filled with _____ inventions and moving parts.

2. The airship had _____ engines that puffed white smoke.

3. The inventor worked on an _____ clock with tiny moving pieces.

4. The scientist adjusted the _____ levers to start the engine.

5. The streets were lined with _____ gadgets and automaton assistants.

107. Fill in the blanks with 'was' or 'were'.

1. The scientist _____ trapped in an alternate reality.

2. There _____ two versions of the same city in different dimensions.

3. A mysterious portal _____ discovered inside the laboratory.

4. The people in this world _____ slightly different from us.

5. _____ this the same planet or a parallel Earth?

108. Rearrange the words to make sentences about parallel universes.

1. world, different, but, looked, same, the, was.

   _____

2. portal, glowing, into, stepped, he, the.

   _____

3. version, alternate, an, of, myself, saw, I.

   _____

4. changed, reality, suddenly, everything.

   _____

5. another, in, world, was, I.

   _____

109. Fill in the blanks with the correct answers.

🐉	it's a	_____
🍌	it's a	_____
🍇	it's a	_____
🍈	it's a	_____
🍋	it's a	_____

110. Fill in the blanks with 'do' or 'does'.

1. _____ aliens exist on distant planets?

2. _____ you believe in intergalactic civilizations?

3. The spaceship _____ not need fuel to travel at light speed.

4. _____ astronauts train for zero gravity?

5. The space station _____ not allow visitors without permission.

111. Rearrange the words to make sentences about cosmic adventures.

1. spaceship, stars, through, the, zoomed.
   _____

2. glowing, planets, sky, filled, the, was, with.
   _____

3. astronauts, far, travelled, galaxy, into.
   _____

4. signals, received, unknown, planet, from, were, an.
   _____

5. mission, the, was, explore, to, deep, space.
   _____

112. Choose the correct word from the list to complete the sentences.

Words:
intergalactic   extraterrestrial   infinite
distant   cosmic   mysterious

1. Scientists detected a _____ signal from a planet beyond our galaxy.

2. The universe is _____, stretching far beyond human understanding.

3. The spaceship prepared for an _____ journey through space.

4. A _____ planet was found orbiting a giant blue star.

5. We might not be alone; _____ life could be out there.

113. List four different edible things.

1. _____ 2. _____

3. _____ 4. _____

114. Circle all the nouns. Then, write them in the space provided.

1. Oliver is carrying a basket of strawberries.
   _____

2. Samantha is baking a chocolate cake.
   _____

3. Daniel received a surprise gift.
   _____

4. He is unwrapping the present excitedly.
   _____

5. Sophia is standing near the lemonade stand.
   _____

6. She is pouring the lemonade into a cup.
   _____

7. Emma bought fresh bananas and apples.
   _____

8. She is peeling the apples for dessert.
   _____

115. Look around and list all the nouns you find in your house:

- _____
- _____
- _____
- _____
- _____

116. Complete each sentence using 'he', 'she', 'it', or 'they'.

a. Jason is holding a football. _____ is about to kick it.

b. Lily picked some wildflowers. _____ is arranging them in a vase.

c. Thomas and his friends are at the park. _____ are playing on the swings.

d. Amelia found a lost kitten. _____ is feeding it some milk.

e. The bicycle has a flat tire. _____ needs to be repaired.

117. Write a synonym (similar meaning) and an antonym (opposite meaning) for each word.

Word	Synonym	Antonym
Happy	_____	_____
Cold	_____	_____
Big	_____	_____
Fast	_____	_____
Strong	_____	_____

118. Look at the picture and write 5 sentences describing it.

- _____
- _____
- _____
- _____
- _____

119. Fill in the blanks using the correct pronoun to replace the noun(s).

1. Daniel is in the kitchen. _____ is making a sandwich.

2. Chloe and Emma love to paint. _____ create beautiful artwork.

3. My dog is sleeping. _____ looks very tired.

4. Joshua is at the park. _____ is playing football.

5. Olivia and I are best friends. _____ always have fun together.

120. Look at the picture and write five sentences describing what you see. Try to use at least one noun, one adjective, and one verb in each sentence.

1. _____
2. _____
3. _____
4. _____
5. _____

121. Rewrite each sentence using correct capital letters, punctuation marks, and grammar.

we went to disneyland last summer

_____

my sister's birthday is in june

_____

are you coming to the party

_____

sarah lives in london

_____

our school library is filled with books

_____

122. Rewrite the sentences in the opposite tense. (Present – Past) or (Past – Present)

He runs to the park.   *He ran to the park.*

They ate their lunch.   _____

She was reading a book.   _____

I write stories for fun.   _____

The cat slept on the sofa.   _____

Challenge:
Write one sentence in future tense on your own.

123. Imagine you had a magic wand. Write a creative paragraph (5–7 sentences) starting with:

"If I had a magic wand, I would

....

....

....

....

....

....

....

Try to use:

- At least one compound sentence
- A simile or a metaphor
- A feeling word (e.g., thrilled, amazed, worried)

124. Underline the adverb (a word that tells us more about the verb) in each sentence.

1. She sings beautifully in the choir.
2. The cat ran quickly up the tree.
3. I always brush my teeth before bed.
4. We will leave soon for the picnic.
5. James spoke softly to the baby.

Now, write a sentence using the adverb "carefully".

....

....

125. Write a short, imaginative dialogue between two friends talking about their favourite hobbies. Use quotation marks, full stops, and question marks correctly.

Start like this:
Alex: Hey Mia, what's your favourite thing to do after school?
Mia: I love...

Write at least 6 lines of conversation

....

....

....

....

....

....

126. Choose the correct preposition from the brackets.

1. The bird is (on / in) the tree.

2. The cat ran (under / over) the table.

3. The car drove (through / between) the tunnel.

4. The book is (beside / inside) the bag.

5. The dog jumped (into / across) the pond.

127. Make each simple sentence longer by adding adjectives, adverbs, and prepositions.

Example:

The cat sleeps.

    The fluffy cat sleeps quietly under the warm blanket.

1. The cat sleeps.

   _____

2. She walks.

   _____

3. He reads a book.

   _____

4. We play outside.

   _____

5. The sun shines.

   _____

128. Rearrange the jumbled words into meaningful and grammatically correct sentences. Remember capital letters and full stops!

1. ice / loves / eat / cream / to / Jack

   _____

2. the / sky / blue / is

   _____

3. runs / fast / dog / the

   _____

4. plays / sister / my / piano / the

   _____

5. book / an / interesting / read / I

   _____

129. Circle or underline the correct word in each sentence.

1. I saw a _____ (bare / bear) in the zoo.

2. The knight wore shiny _____ (armor / armour).

3. We will _____ (meet / meat) at the park.

4. Please _____ (write / right) your name on the form.

5. He climbed to the top of the _____ (peak / peek).

130. Look at the picture and write a 5–7 sentence story about the lost puppy.

Think about:

How the puppy got lost
Who found it
What happened next
How it felt

....
....
....
....
....
....
....

131. List five words for each category.

- Fruits: ....

- Animals: ....

- Colours: ....

- Shapes: ....

- Weather: ....

132. Draw a line to match each word with its opposite (antonym).

Word		Antonym
Hot	• •	Dark
Soft	• •	Cold
Happy	• •	Slow
Light	• •	Hard
Fast	• •	Sad

133. Now write a sentence using any one antonym from question no. 132.

_____

134. Write a word that rhymes with each of the following:

- Cat → _____

- Ball → _____

- Tree → _____

- Star → _____

- Boat → _____

135. Each word below hides another smaller word. Find and write the hidden word.

- Sunflower → _____
- Notebook → _____
- Butterfly → _____
- Strawberry → _____
- Raincoat → _____

136. Look at the picture and write a story.

_____
_____
_____
_____
_____
_____
_____
_____
_____
_____

137. Fill in a synonym (similar meaning) and an antonym (opposite meaning) for each word.

Word	Synonym	Antonym
Brave	_____	_____
Bright	_____	_____
Tired	_____	_____
Gentle	_____	_____
Hard	_____	_____

138. Use each synonym in a new sentence.

....

....

....

....

....

....

....

139. Reading Comprehension: "The Lost Kitten"

Passage:

Sophia was walking home from school when she heard a soft meowing. She looked around and found a tiny kitten hiding behind a bush. It was shivering in the cold. Sophia carefully picked it up and carried it home. She gave it some milk and wrapped it in a warm blanket. The kitten purred happily.

Questions:

1. Where did Sophia find the kitten?

   _____

2. How was the kitten feeling?

   _____

3. What did Sophia do for the kitten?

   _____

4. What sound did the kitten make?

   _____

5. What do you think happened next? (Use your imagination!)

   _____

   _____

   _____

   _____

   _____

140. Correct the capitalisation, grammar, and punctuation in these sentences.

1. yesterday we visited my uncle in new york

   _____

2. emily loves to eat chocolate cake

   _____

3. do you want to play football with us

   _____

4. my brother and i went to the park on sunday

   _____

5. the sun is shining brightly in the sky

   _____

141. Write a funny sentence using alliteration — where most words start with the same letter.

Example:
Fiona found five funny frogs.

- B: _____
- C: _____
- D: _____
- S: _____
- T: _____

142. **Write a 4-line rhyming poem about your favourite season.**

Example for Spring:

"Flowers bloom beneath the sun,

Breezy days are full of fun.

Birds return and rivers sing,

What a joy it is — sweet Spring!"

Your Turn:

_____

_____

_____

_____

143. **Circle the compound words (words made from two smaller words) in each sentence.**

1. Olivia put her notebook on the table.

2. We saw a firefly glowing in the dark.

3. The sunflower swayed in the wind.

4. The football match was exciting.

5. I used a toothbrush before going to bed.

144. Invent a superhero and fill in the details below:

- Name: _____

- Superpowers: _____

- What they fight for: _____

- Costume description: _____

145. Fill in the missing vowels to complete each word.

1. C _ r   (a vehicle)   → _____

2. B _ _ k   (something you read)   → _____

3. P _ _ c _ l (something you write with)   → _____

4. S _ _ o _ l (a place to learn)   → _____

146. Put each word into the correct category: Person, Place, or Thing.

Word	Person	Place	Thing
Doctor			
Library			
Pencil			
Farmer			
Mountain			

147. Fantasy Writing: Magical Adventure

Write a short story (5–7 sentences) about a magical land, a prince or princess, and a special adventure.

Try to include:
A problem or mystery, something magical (object, animal, place), a surprising ending

_____
_____
_____
_____
_____
_____
_____

148. Do as instructed.

Part 1: Draw a line to match the correct vowel with the picture:

A/a	• •	cupcake
E/e	• •	umbrella
I/i	• •	apple
O/o	• •	earth
U/u	• •	orange

Part 2: Use each word in a simple sentence.

For example:

Apple – I ate a red apple.

Now your turn:

1. Apple: _____

2. Earth: _____

3. Ice Cream: _____

4. Orange: _____

5. Umbrella: _____

149. Draw your own mystical creature, then write four descriptive sentences about it.

Think about:

What it looks like - Where it lives - What powers it has - What it eats

150. Do as instructed.

(a) Draw a line between the weather word and its correct meaning.

Weather Word	Meaning
Snowy •	• Lots of sunshine
Cloudy •	• Water falling from the sky
Sunny •	• Strong air moving fast
Windy •	• White flakes falling from the sky
Rainy •	• The sky is covered in clouds

(b) Which is your favourite weather and why?

Snowy

Rainy

Summer

Windy

Stormy

Sunny

_____

_____

151. Read the sentence and answer the question.

Sentence:

"The children ran through the field, their laughter filling the air."

Question:

a. What were the children doing?

_____

_____

b. Describe what the field might look like using your imagination!

_____

_____

152. Circle the word that does NOT belong in each group.

1. Apple   Banana   Chair   Mango
2. Pencil   Notebook   Spoon   Eraser
3. Cat   Dog   Fish   Table
4. Shirt   Shoes   Hat   Car
5. Blue   Red   Yellow   Elephant

153. Write a 5–6 sentence letter to yourself five years from now. Tell future-you what you hope to achieve, learn, and remember.

Start like this:

Dear Future Me,

_____

_____

_____

_____

Love,

Your Present Self

Tips:
Mention your dreams, goals, and something fun you love right now!

154. Count the number of syllables (beats in a word) for each word.

1. Butterfly → _____ syllables
2. Elephant → _____ syllables
3. Chair → _____ syllables
4. Exciting → _____ syllables
5. Watermelon → _____ syllables

155. Reading Comprehension: "A Trip to the Zoo"

Passage:

Liam and his family went to the zoo on Saturday. They saw lions, tigers, and monkeys. Liam loved watching the penguins waddle and swim. They had lunch near the giraffe enclosure and then bought souvenirs from the gift shop.

Answer the questions:

Where did Liam and his family go?

_____

What animals did they see?

_____

Which animal did Liam enjoy watching the most?

_____

Where did they eat lunch?

_____

What did they do at the end of their visit?

_____

156. Underline the adjective in each sentence.

1. The sky was a beautiful shade of blue.

2. Noah wore a thick jacket on the snowy day.

3. Sophia's dog is very playful.

4. We sat on a comfortable couch.

5. The delicious pizza smelled amazing.

157. Rewrite the sentences using proper punctuation and capital letters.

1. my dad and i went to paris last summer

   _____

2. do you like ice cream

   _____

3. we had a picnic in the park on sunday

   _____

4. my birthday is in december

   _____

5. lucy loves playing football

   _____

158. Complete each simile with a fun and fitting comparison.

1. As fast as a _____
2. As light as a _____
3. As quiet as a _____
4. As strong as a _____
5. As bright as a _____

159. Draw a line to connect the matching homophones (words that sound the same but have different meanings).

Word 1	Word 2
See	Flower
Pair	Sea
Brake	Won
Flour	Pear
One	Break

160. Spot the things that Start with 'B' and name them.

161. Write a humorous short conversation between a pirate and their chatty parrot.

Example start:
Pirate: "Ahoy, Polly! Where's me treasure map?"
Parrot: "Squawk! You used it to cover yer soup, Cap'n!"
Your turn:

_____

_____

_____

_____

_____

162. Choose the correct option to complete the sentence.

1. It's important to brush your teeth _____ a day.
   a. twise   b. twice   c. twisee

2. Birds use their _____ to fly.
   a. wings   b. wengs   c. winngs

3. Dolphins are known to be very _____ animals.
   a. intelijent   b. intelligent   c. intelligennt

4. The baby _____ cried for its mother.
   a. dear   b. deer   c. deir

5. Mount Everest is the _____ mountain in the world.
   a. tallist   b. tallest   c. taallest

6. Bees make _____ from flowers.
   a. honey   b. hunny   c. honee

163. Complete these sentences with the correct prepositions:

Word Bank:
above   behind   beside   near   in front of
below   over   under   between   along

1. The cabbages are growing _____ the carrots.
2. The house is _____ the path.
3. The trees are _____ the garden.
4. The flowers bloom _____ the edge of the walkway.
5. The clouds float _____ the sky.

164. Change each sentence from present tense to past tense.

1. I eat a sandwich.
   _____
2. She drinks orange juice.
   _____
3. They enjoy the cake.
   _____

165. Look at each picture and write the action verb shown.

1. _____ 2. _____ 3. _____ 4. _____

Word Bank:
cook   eat   wash   serve

166. Write one complete sentence using each verb in the present tense.

1. Cook _____
2. Serve _____
3. Eat _____
4. Wash _____

167. Rewrite the following sentence in the past tense:

Sentence: He washes the dishes.

Rewrite: _____

Now rewrite this past tense sentence in the present tense:

Sentence: He cooked pasta for lunch.

Rewrite: _____

168. Circle whether each sentence is in the past or present tense.

1. He cooks dinner with his dad. — Past / Present
2. He ate all the pizza! — Past / Present
3. He serves the food to his friends. — Past / Present
4. He washed the dishes after lunch. — Past / Present

169. Fill in the blanks using the correct prepositions.

1. The fire is _____ the two sitting scouts.
2. The log is _____ the boy's legs.
3. The flag is _____ the girl's hand.
4. The marshmallows are _____ the sticks.
5. The scouts are sitting _____ the fire.

Word Bank:
beside   in   between   on   in front of   beneath

170. Imagine what actions can happen with these objects. Write a verb (action word) for each noun.

1. Book   _____
2. Pen   _____
3. Plant   _____

171. Fill in the blanks using prepositions that match the picture.

1. The pen is lying _____ the table.

2. The plant is _____ the stack of books.

3. The top book is placed _____ all the others.

4. The bookmarks are hanging _____ the pages.

Word Bank:
on   under   over   beside   between   inside

172. Read each sentence carefully and replace the underlined noun(s) with the correct pronoun.

1. Maya is reading a mystery novel. _____ enjoys solving puzzles.

2. Leo and Arjun play guitar together. _____ sound amazing as a duo.

3. The kitten is hiding under the bed. _____ doesn't want to come out.

4. Ava is watering the plants. _____ loves gardening.

5. You and I are baking cookies. _____ make a great team!

Use the correct pronouns like:
he, she, it, we, they.

173. Draw a line to match each body part with what it helps you do.

 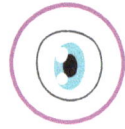   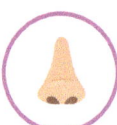

174. Read each sentence. Identify its tense, then rewrite it in the other two tenses.

Sentence 1. Birds chirp in the morning.
Rewrite in Other Tenses

_____
_____

Sentence 2. We planted trees last week.
Rewrite in Other Tenses

_____
_____

Sentence 3. She will water the garden tomorrow.
Rewrite in Other Tenses

_____
_____

175. Complete each sentence with the most suitable preposition from the word bank.

Word Bank:
under   behind   above   across   near   beside   through   around

1. The squirrel ran _____ the tree trunk.

2. The sun peeked out from _____ the clouds.

3. A butterfly fluttered _____ the flowers.

4. The rabbit hid _____ the bush.

5. A narrow stream flows _____ the meadow.

6. The beehive is hanging _____ the branch.

7. My tent is set up _____ the big oak tree.

176. Write 3–5 descriptive sentences about the picture. Use adjectives, prepositions, and action words.

Example:

A sleepy cat is lying on a wooden shelf. It looks calm and peaceful. Beside the cat, there is a red pot with a green leafy plant. The cat's tail stretches behind it, and one paw hangs down lazily.

Now you try:

1. _____
2. _____
3. _____
4. _____
5. _____

177. Colour them as shown.

178. Identify the five senses.

_____   _____   _____   _____   _____

Word bank:
Sight   Smell   Touch   Hearing   Taste

179. **Look closely at what the children are doing. Fill in the blanks with the correct action verb.**

Word Bank:
building   digging   smiling   playing   holding

1. The girl is _____ a red bucket.

2. They are _____ a tall sandcastle together.

3. Both children are _____ happily.

4. They are _____ at the beach.

180. **Choose 4 things from the picture and describe each with two adjectives.**

Example: Duck → small, cheerful

1. Elephant   →   _____, _____

2. Tree   →   _____, _____

3. Pond   →   _____, _____

4. Sky   →   _____, _____

181. Look outside your window or imagine a scene. Write five descriptive sentences about the weather today.

Try to include:

- Temperature
- Sky appearance
- Sounds or smells
- How it makes you feel
- What people or animals are doing

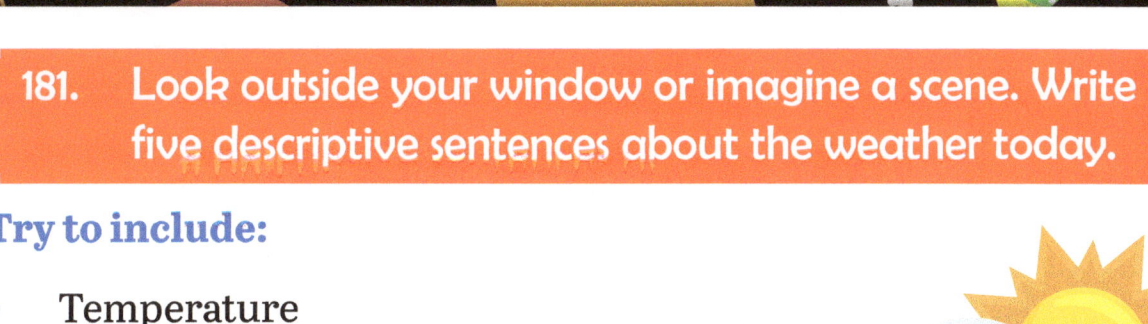

_____
_____
_____
_____
_____

182. Write a two-line poem where both lines rhyme.

Example:

"The stars above shine oh so bright,
They twinkle softly through the night."

Your poem:

_____
_____

Instruction:
Try rhyming words like light/night   play/day   smile/style

183. Circle the verb (action word) in each sentence.

1. Lucas runs to the store.

2. Mia sings beautifully.

3. The dog sleeps in the sun.

4. We watched a movie last night.

5. The baby crawls on the floor.

184. Put the jumbled words in the correct order to form a complete sentence.

1. loves / music / playing / she

   _____

2. tree / the / squirrel / climbed / the

   _____

3. ice cream / favourite / is / my / dessert

   _____

4. dog / barking / the / is / loudly

   _____

5. my / reads / father / newspaper / the

   _____

185. Write three – four sentences to describe your own house or your friend's.

Think about:
- Location (on a hill, in a forest, by the sea?)
- What makes it special?
- What colour or shape is it?

_____

_____

_____

_____

186. Write a thank-you note to your teacher, expressing your appreciation.

Start like this:
Dear Teacher,

_____

_____

_____

_____

Sincerely,

_____

Tips:
Mention something you enjoyed learning this year!

187. Change each sentence into the past tense.

1. I play in the garden.

   _____

2. She eats an apple.

   _____

3. They walk to school.

   _____

4. The bird sings in the tree.

   _____

5. We run in the race.

   _____

188. Write the first word that comes to your mind when you read the following:

- Sun   →   _____

- Book   →   _____

- Water   →   _____

- Ice   →   _____

- Balloon →   _____

189. Mention a story/ book and write why you love it.

_____
_____
_____
_____
_____
_____
_____

190. Observe the picture carefully and answer the questions.

1. Where does the dragon live?

   _____

2. What magical spell is the wizard casting?

   _____

3. Why is the unicorn standing near the castle?

   _____

4. Is something mysterious happening?

   _____

191. Find three smaller words inside each big word.

- Strawberry → _____, _____, _____
- Lighthouse → _____, _____, _____
- Playground → _____, _____, _____

192. Do you like dogs or cats more? Write five things you love about your pet!

_____
_____
_____
_____
_____
_____

193. Write a short story (5–6 sentences) after observing the picture.

_____
_____
_____
_____
_____
_____

194. **Observe the scene carefully:**

- Students are at their desk
- A teacher stands by the blackboard
- A school bag is on the floor

Now, imagine what happens next and write a short story (6–8 sentences).

You could think about:

- Is the student about to ask a question?
- Is the teacher about to reveal a surprise lesson?
- Did someone forget their homework?

_____
_____
_____
_____
_____
_____
_____

195. **Look at the picture carefully. Then, fill in the blanks with the correct part of speech.**

1. Can you spot 3 nouns in the picture?

   _____
   _____
   _____

2. Pick 3 adjectives to describe what you see.

   _____
   _____
   _____

3. What is the horse or chicken doing? Name 2 actions.

   _____
   _____

196. **Look at the picture and fill in the missing letter.**

 ____pple    ____ear

 ____anana    ____uck

 ____arrot    ____ish

197. Find the missing letter.

happ_   i / e / y   _ngry   e / a / w

sa_   f / d / t   shock_d   e / s / i

in lov_   e / a / f

198. "IGHT" Sounding Words – Fill in the blanks with the correct words.

Word Bank:
fright   flight   light   right

1. We turn on a lamp to get some _____ at night.

2. A bird can take _____ in the sky.

3. The opposite of left is _____.

4. I had a bad dream and woke up from a _____.

199. Choose the correct word from the pair to complete each sentence.

1. I saw a black _____ behind the tree. (bare / bear)
2. Please throw the trash over _____. (their / there)
3. She wants to _____ a beautiful dress. (wear / where)
4. He hurt his _____ while playing football. (toe / tow)
5. My brother will _____ the story for me. (read / reed)
6. We watched the sun _____ behind the hills. (sail / set)

200. Look at the picture and list all the nouns you can see.

1. _____
2. _____
3. _____
4. _____
5. _____
6. _____
7. _____
8. _____

201. Unscrable the words below.

 QUIMOSOT _____   TARECPILALR _____

 RAGFLYDON _____   FUTLYBTER _____

 TEBEEL _____   WPAS _____

 TOHM _____   ACROHOCCK _____